Porridge the Tartan Cat

To Kate and Isla, who now have a tartan cat.
How cool is that? Me-wow – A.D.

To my lovely parents Mark and Galina – Y.S.

Young Kelpies is an imprint of Floris Books
First published in 2017 by Floris Books
Text © 2017 Alan Dapré. Illustrations © 2017 Floris Books
Alan Dapré and Yuliya Somina have asserted their rights
under the Copyright, Designs and Patent Act 1988 to
be identified as the Author and Illustrator of this work

The publisher acknowledges subsidy from
Creative Scotland towards the publication
of this volume

MIX
Paper from
responsible sources
FSC
www.fsc.org   FSC® C117931

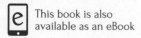

This book is also
available as an eBook

British Library CIP data available
ISBN 978-178250-355-2
Printed & bound by MBM Print SCS Ltd, Glasgow

Porridge the Tartan Cat
and the Brawsome Bagpipes

Written by Alan Dapré

Illustrated by Yuliya Somina

Young Kelpies

Tickle me under the chin
and you can read it too.

You can even put your
name here, for now:

_____

_____

 **Me-ow!**

1

Porridge Says Hi

Hi, I'm Porridge the Tartan Cat.

I bet you've never seen a tartan cat before. When I was a wee kitten I toppled into a tin of tartan paint, which is easy to do and not so easy to say.

Toppled into a tin of tartan paint.

Toppled into a tin of tartan paint.

Now, us cats don't like getting wet, so there was

no way I was going to wash it off. Or lick it off.

Me-yuck!

So that's how I became the world's first and only tartan cat. I'm quite famous round here. Lots of people give me a wave, or better still, stop to tickle my tartan ears.

I live by Loch Loch in a rambling old house with the fabulous McFun family. I'm very kind to them. I let them feed me fishy biscuits and sit with me by the warm fire. Och, I like the McFun family so much I've even given them names.

There's Gadget Grandad, Groovy Gran, Mini Mum, Dino Dad, Roaring Ross and Invisible Isla. I call them the Big Yins and I have a fab and funny story to tell you about each and every one of them. Aye, I've *cat*-a-logged all their braw adventures for you.

So why not have a read? Gadget Grandad is up first. I'll sit here with you and have a wee catnap while you enjoy it.

Me-yawn

2

Snoring Sunday

Some say it all began one dark and stormy night when the wind was howling like a cat with an empty food bowl...

But actually, it all began one sunny Sunday just after breakfast and this full stop. The twins were getting ready to spend another boring Sunday at their grandparents' house. All Grandad did there was snore all day.

Snore. Snore. Snore. Snore. Snore. Snore. Snore.

I'm getting bored just telling you about it.

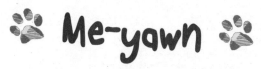

Me-yawn

The twins – Isla and Ross – were born at exactly the same time as me. Porridge. You know, *the* Tartan Cat. And that makes us all the same age in human years. But I'm about six times older and wiser in cat years. Cats like me are *very* wise indeed. You never see us chasing after dogs or burying bones in wet cement. And we never ever say daft things like "Woof!"

Me-oops

I just did.

I tried to cheer up Isla and Ross by batting them
a football with my tartan tail. They headed it to each
other near the freezer, looking very cool. *Freezing*, in
fact. Ross shivered as he shut the freezer door.

🐾 Me-oops 🐾

I'd left it open when I got out a tasty fish lolly.

 Me-yum

Both of the twins are way better at football than me, even though we have the same number of legs. I *can* dribble a bit... especially when I think of fishy biscuits.

Mmmm. Fishy biscuits.

Mum was in another room, walking in circles on the phone. (Last time I did that I fell off!) After the call ended, she came into the kitchen.

"That was Grandad," she said brightly. "He wants you both to stay not just today, but *all week* while Gran is away on a cookery course."

Isla froze, even though the freezer door was shut. The football bounced into the bin and catapulted two wet teabags towards me. Ross dived and caught one, like a nimble ninja cat. (I'm a nimble ninja cat too. One day you'll see – or maybe you won't because I'm so nimble!)

"But that's like a *week* of boring snoring Sundays!" groaned Ross. "Can't I stay here and Porridge go instead?"

"Porridge is a cat," sighed Mum, taking the other teabag off my head. "And you both know Grandad is allergic to cats."

"I wish he was allergic to twins," grumbled Isla.

3

The Funny Chapter
Where Not Much Happens

Now I don't like being left out, unless it's being left out all night so I can chase dozy mice. So when the twins were driven to Grandad's house for the week, I followed, full of curiosity and breakfast.

First I jumped onto a low brick wall. Then I leapt into a tree and bravely tiptoed across its bendy branches. Twelve trees, seven lampposts, three street signs, two puddles *and* a poodle later I was standing in front of a red door.

Mum's car spluttered to a stop by the gate and I spluttered too as I darted under an upside-down flowerpot, just in time.

Grandad opened the front door, his face full of joy (and his flowerpot full of cat). He greeted the twins with a jaunty tune on his tartan bagpipes.

Isla and Ross (and one flowerpot) pottered through the door, while the old man tottered into his boring old lounge to lounge in his boring old armchair.

"Lovely to have you here, and you too Porridge," said Grandad, peering over his glasses. "My new anti-sneezing specs will come in very handy, or should I say nosy, today."

How did he know I was here?

"Porridge! Your tail is sticking out through the

hole in the flower pot!" laughed Isla.

I cheekily shrugged off the flowerpot and stretched on the carpet, feeling quite at home not at home.

"I think I'll have a wee nap," the weary old man muttered, hugging his bagpipes like a tartan teddy. "I suggest you three take it easy today and have an early night. Things are going to get pretty crazy around here tomorrow."

The twins didn't believe that one bit.

Now, talking of crazy things, the room was full of them. Grandad is always tinkering away at something in his shed. That's why we call him Gadget Grandad. You can call him that too. He won't mind.

Today the house was so full of gadgets that there was no room to swing a cat!

Me-phew

Ross stumbled over a strange silver machine with levers and letters and stubbed his toe.

Me-owch

"Is that a typewriter?" he said, rubbing his toe.

"It's a tripewriter," said Gadget Grandad, slyly grinning like a quick brown fox. "You type in any old tripe and out comes something sensible. I used to use it for my homework at school. Try it."

Ross randomly tapped the keys without looking. A wee silver bell rang and a neatly typed sheet of paper scrolled out.

Sharks never run out of teeth because whenever one is lost a new tooth rolls into place.

"I didn't know that," said Ross, impressed.

It sounded fishy to me but Gadget Grandad said it was true. I leapt on the sofa and accidentally sat on a TV remote control.

A cookery programme for kids appeared on the screen. The cook was bustling about making a lemon drizzle cake.

"Take a sniff," chuckled Gadget Grandad.

As soon as we did, our noses tingled with the zesty zing of fresh lemons.

"That's actually impossible," gasped Isla.

"That's actually my SmellyVision," said Gadget Grandad. "Whatever you see on the screen, you smell it too. Even if it's a stinky old dug."

Me-yuck

Ross and Isla hunted for more gadgets.

"This looks like an uninteresting umbrella," Ross whispered, about to open it.

"A fantastic Funbrella actually," said Gadget Grandad. "*Never* open it in the house."

"Why? Do you get bad luck?" asked Isla.

"You get spun into the sky. It's great fun, until the wind turns it inside oot."

Ross put it down quickly.

"And what's this?" said Isla, holding up a slipper.

"That's a slipper," grunted Gadget Grandad, his eyes closing sleepily. Within a second he was snoring. And this chapter got really boring. SO BORING we're going straight to another one. *Come on!*

4

Revenge!

We tiptoed quietly, trying not to wake Gadget Grandad.

Then Ross accidentally tripped over an empty flowerpot (I wonder how *that* got there?) and landed on a pile of yellow newspapers.

"These newspapers are older than me," said Ross.

"They're older than all of us put together!" said Isla, peering at a crumpled front page.

There was a picture of a small boy in long shorts, holding up a trophy the size of a small boy in long shorts, holding up a trophy the size of a small boy

in long shorts, holding up a trophy the size of a...
Och, you get the picture.

"That's me," said Gadget Grandad, waking up
again. "I got the school Dux."

"Your school had pet ducks?" asked Ross.

Gadget Grandad chuckled. "No, I mean D-u-x, a prize for doing well in class. Though we had pet ducks too. You're not the first to confuse them. On that fateful day my arch-enemy Fergus McFungus dived into the school pond and nabbed the school ducks, thinking he was stealing the prize off me. They pooped everywhere! Everyone laughed and Fergus stormed out, shouting, 'Yuck!' and 'Revenge!' That's him scowling behind me in the photo."

"I didn't know you had an arch-enemy," said Isla.

"Aye, Fergus McFungus and I have been rivals for as long as I can remember. Back then he was thin as a toadstool stalk," said Gadget Grandad. "He wore a long coat and always had a spotted toadstool in his cap! Och, and *very* sticky fingers. So sticky that everything he touched he kept forever…"

The twins wanted to know more, but the old man fell fast asleep again. Really fast – like in a *nanosecond*. (Not to be confused with a *nanasecond*, which is really slow, and is exactly as long as your nana takes to walk to the shops and back.)

"I'm mega-bored already," sighed Ross.

"And me," huffed Isla. "I hope it's not like this all week!"

Things stayed mega-boring until a smart watch beside Gadget Grandad started to ʙʟᴇᴇᴘ. The twins ʙʟᴇᴇᴘ took it **ʙʟᴇᴇᴘ** into the **ʙʟᴇᴇᴘ** kitchen so **ʙʟᴇᴇᴘ** it wouldn't **ʙʟᴇᴇᴘ** wake Gadget **ʙʟᴇᴇᴘ** Grandad.

There was a text message on the screen.

THE STINKY
SCOTCH PIES
ARE OFF

What stinky Scotch pies? If any food was off

I would have smelt it already.

 **Me-sniff!**

There were no pies anywhere. The kitchen oven

said zero degrees, which meant it hadn't been turned

on or gone to university.

"Who sent the message?" asked Ross.

"Groovy Gran?" guessed Isla. "She *is* on a cookery course."

"Naw, she only makes tattie scones," said Ross.

True. Whenever she tried to bake something else, she always ended up with traditional tattie scones.

Hmmm. So if Gran hadn't sent the message, who had? My pal Basil once said, "Always sleep on a big problem – and a big bed – until breakfast."

Good advice. So I curled up for a nap and hoped Monday morning would bring the answer, along with a bowl of fishy biscuits.

By the time you get to Chapter 5 it will be Monday. *Magic.*

5

Magic Monday

Gadget Grandad put hot porridge on the breakfast table. The kind of porridge you can eat. Not me – I'm cool Porridge. So cool I've got my own tartan clothing range. Available in all good pet shops.

"I'm sorry yesterday was boring," he said. "I was waiting in for a message. It didnae come."

Ross dropped his mouth open.

Isla dropped her spoon on the floor.

I dropped into the sink.

Me-splash!

It wasn't very cool of me to fall off a windowsill.
So let's not talk about it ever again.

Ever.

Again.

"But a message *did* come," said Ross. "You were asleep
and we didn't want to wake you." He scooped up the
watch and eagerly showed Gadget Grandad the message.

THE STINKY SCOTCH PIES ARE OFF

The old man leapt from his chair and darted around the kitchen, grabbing his battered hat and long black coat. "That message was sent by my robotic spy-in-the-sky. Let's go. We have no time to lose!"

He scooped his bagpipes under one arm, and slipped on his dark glasses. I slipped on a bar of soap and fell in the sink again. Shh! Don't tell anyone. *Not even me.*

"See you later, Porridge," said Isla.

No way, I meowed. Tartan cats don't like to miss out.

"What are we doing?" asked Ross, as he shouldered his surprisingly heavy rucksack. (*It was full of Porridge, heh heh.*)

Gadget Grandad waved his fingers like wrinkled wands and whispered mysteriously, "Wait and see!"

6
It's Only Me!

A short while later, we boarded the number 37 bus.

We had to stand all the way into town because the bus was full. Mainly full of an elephant called Basil, who lived with Mavis Muckle – the twins' next-door neighbour.

Mavis loved animals and they loved her. Any creature who strayed into her home was welcome. *Even me.* I loved Mavis and her cat flap. It led straight to a bowl of fishy biscuits.

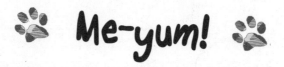 Me-yum!

When the bus arrived at the park, Grandad took the twins to a bench nearby. As they sat down, he checked it for bugs that might secretly listen to what he was about to say.

No bugs, I meowed, shooing away a nosy ladybird.

Hearing me, Ross held up his rucksack. "I think we have company."

Gadget Grandad opened the bag and stuck his head inside. He let out a sneeze, and then a cat.

"What are you doing in there?" he said, with a smile.

Hiding, of course!

"It's too late to take you home," said Gadget
Grandad. "We're on a mission. *THE STINKY SCOTCH
PIES ARE OFF* is a secret coded message."

"What does it mean?" asked Isla.

"The 'Scotch pies' are *spies*. They are 'off' to a hidden location where they will start plotting to destroy the world. **AND VOLCANOES. AND FISHY BISCUITS. AND ELEPHANTS.** Unless we stop them!"

"That does sound stinky," said Ross.

"The spies belong to a secret secret organisation called **S.P.L.O.T.** It's short for **S**pies. **P**lotting. **L**ots. **O**f. **T**rouble." Gadget Grandad sighed. "Really bad secret secrets go into the Chief Splotter's recipe book – *The Splotter's Guide To Cooking Up Trouble*. Only one copy of the book exists, and it can only be read once a year. Fergus McFungus is planning on stealing it. Today."

"Your arch-enemy Fergus?" asked Isla.

"Aye," said Grandad. "He once tried to copy the secret secret recipe book. But he was caught and thrown out of **S.P.L.O.T.** Now he seeks revenge.

AND THE BOOK. **AND WORLD DESTRUCTION. AND PROBABLY LOTS OF OTHER BAD THINGS I CAN'T REMEMBER AT THE MOMENT!"**

 Me-HELP!

7

The Secret Secret Chapter

"Everyone hold on to my coat. We must fly," said Gadget Grandad. He blew hard into his bagpipes, and then something amazing happened! Three long pipes swung out and up from the swelling tartan bag and whirled overhead like helicopter blades.

CHUK-CHUK-CHUK

We rose into the air, high above Tattiebogle Town and Loch Loch.

"This is megamazincredibrill!" cried Ross. "Why are we up here?"

"So we can spot the spies more easily. They like to wear big kilts and frowns," shouted Gadget Grandad. He squeezed air from his bagpipes and we swooped down low. "Fergus has been up to no good ever since we were kids. I keep trying to stop his fiendish plots but he's more slippery than a buttered slug."

"There's a spy," said Isla, spotting a man in a
big kilt when we buzzed over a busy market. "And
another. And another! Wait, they can't *all* be spies..."

"Hmmm, kilts must be very popular in Tattiebogle
just now," said Grandad.

I jabbed my tail at a big sign.

"This could be trickier than we thought," groaned
Gadget Grandad. "Keep your eyes peeled for Fergus
McFungus."

"He'll have a toadstool in his cap," remembered Ross.

"I see him!" cried Isla, pointing down at Loch Loch, where a man in a long coat was racing a hovercraft across the water.

Without warning, a wild gust of wind turned the whirling bagpipes upside down and we plummeted towards the cold, choppy loch.

"Do something!" shouted Ross.

Gadget Grandad pulled a toy boat from his pocket.

"How will we all fit in that?" asked Isla.

"Just add water!" Gadget Grandad threw the boat towards the loch below. There was a wee whistling sound then a tiny splosh and a big

wHUMPHF

and the toy boat was suddenly a large rubber dinghy!

One by one, the three Big Yins landed on its big rubbery bottom. I tucked in my claws and landed on my big rubbery bottom too!

With all of us aboard, Gadget Grandad used his bagpipes as a motor and we twanged across the water like a rubber band.

"Where is McFungus going?" Isla shouted above the noise.

"I suspect he's headed towards the secret, mysterious, volcanic island with no name, which spies like to call *The Secret, Mysterious, Volcanic Island With No Name*," answered Gadget Grandad.

8

The Secret, Mysterious Chapter With No Name

(because I can't think of one)

"Follow me," yelled Gadget Grandad, leaping onto the pebbled island shore.

Breathless and excited, we scrambled up a steep slope and keeked over the edge of a volcanic crater.

Hunched together in its secret sunken centre, on an outcrop above a lake of molten lava, were twelve spies dressed in kilts. Among them was the Chief

Splotter, a wiry man with a splotty – I mean spotty – bag. He reached into it and solemnly plucked out *The Splotter's Guide To Cooking Up Trouble*. Its golden cover sparkled in the sunlight and the spies had to put on dark sunglasses to look at it (except one, who had to squint a lot).

Just then, we saw Fergus McFungus spring onto the rim of the crater opposite. He gave Gadget Grandad a cheeky wave.

"We can't let him nab the book or it'll be a recipe for disaster," Gadget Grandad groaned.

"We've got to do something," urged Isla.

Gadget Grandad removed his wristwatch and straightened its silver strap into an aerial. Then he gave the stubby winder button a quick tap and sent his bagpipes whirring on their own, high above them.

Turning his watch left and right, Gadget Grandad manoeuvred the bagpipes above the huddle of spies and then tapped on a different button marked BLOW.

Now the bagpipes blared a catchy toe-tapping tune and the spies got up and danced a reel in dizzy circles, unable to run away or do 'Strip The Willow' properly.

"We'll soon reel them in," chuckled Gadget Grandad. He pressed the button marked SUCK. "Let's catch those windbags in my windbag."

One by one, the spies were sucked from their socks and up into the whirling bagpipes. Seeing the danger, the Chief Splotter dropped the recipe book, but before he could run he was sucked up with a satisfying **shhclooop.**

"Turn up the power!" urged the twins, seeing *The Splotter's Guide To Cooking Up Trouble* spinning towards Fergus McFungus.

"I can't. It's up to full!" Gadget Grandad groaned. "And my bagpipes are full up too!"

He pressed another button marked QUACK, which sent his eye-in-the-sky, a flying spying gadget disguised as a duck, speeding towards us like a bullet.

Here was my chance to get the recipe book and be a hero and win a medal. Or at least get a fishy biscuit. I bent low, tensed my legs and

 **Me-twangggg!**

catapulted myself towards the robot duck.

"Great shot!" yelled Gadget Grandad as I plopped on its back. The downy duck

ducked

down

under my weight and we crazily whirled to the crater rim. I sprang like a tartan tiger and batted the flapping book of secrets away from Fergus McFungus's reach. The book fluttered down into the crater, but not before his sticky fingers tore out a single page.

"Just what I wanted!" crowed Fergus, skipping out of sight, because he was happy – and had a handy skipping rope in his pocket.

I dropped like a stone (or maybe a scone, depending on how you say it), but dug my claws into the crater edge to stop myself from falling into the molten lava. There was nothing I could do but swing from the rim like a tartan toilet freshener.

"Someone save Porridge!" shouted Gadget Grandad.

The Big Yins began skirting around the crater in a brave bid to rescue me.

"We've got 3.4 seconds before he falls," calculated Isla. "Jump!"

She gave her brother a swift shove...

Ross flew forwards...

My claws slipped...

Ross grabbed my paw and I swung below him like a furry pendulum.

"Up you come," said Ross. "Well done, Porridge. You stopped Fergus from getting the whole book!"

"You were very brave," cooed Isla.

A passing pigeon cooed back, flying in formation with the gadget duck.

Mmmm. Pigeon.

"But Fergus will still stir up a pot of trouble with that one ripped-out recipe," sighed Gadget Grandad. "If only I knew which one it was." His shoulders slumped.

"Cheer up, Grandad. Today was way better than a boring snoring Sunday," said Ross, hugging the old man.

"It's not over yet. There's one more thing to do," said Gadget Grandad, waggling his watch. He jabbed

a button marked MUTE and the brawsome bagpipes soared off with a belly full of scotch pies...
I mean spies.

"Where are they going?" asked Isla.

"I'll pop them somewhere they won't be able to talk," said Gadget Grandad, with a wink. "The library!"

9
Terrific Tuesday

Tuesday morning arrived with a sunny smile on its face that brightened everyone's day.

It was time for breakfast. Fishy biscuits swimming in a sea of milk.

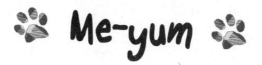 **Me-yum**

I was fishing out my last fish when Gadget Grandad came into the kitchen wearing a suit. A dazzling yellow wetsuit!

"What do you think?" he asked brightly.

"It's very yellow," said Isla, pouring milk into her cereal while she looked at Gadget Grandad.

Ross gave a big sigh. "I wish *I* had a wetsuit."

"Why?" asked Isla.

"Because you're tipping milk in my lap!"

"Oh! Sorry," giggled Isla, only about 97% sorry. Gadget Grandad handed Ross a beach towel.

"What are you doing today?" asked Ross, drying himself.

"Walter-skiing!" whooped Gadget Grandad.

"Water-skiing?" asked Ross, thinking this really wasn't what Grandad was like on Sundays.

"No, *Walter*-skiing," said Gadget Grandad. "It's far more fun. I do it every Tuesday. Today, we need to hurry to the beach, because a little birdie tells me Fergus McFungus is planning a splash-and-grab raid on my Walter-skiing fans. He must be stopped!"

It was all sounding very mysterious.

And wet.

Cats don't do wet.

10

Walter

Down on the rocky beach, Gadget Grandad put on a pair of goggles with clever wee wipers to rub the salty spray away. He pressed a button on his flippers and they doubled in length. Then he picked up his bagpipes and flip-flop-flapped towards the choppy waves.

Everyone was fine with me coming along this time. I'd been such a hero on that crater the day before.

"Where's Fergus?" asked Ross.

"I think he's hiding at the whale-weigh station (get it?) out at sea," said Gadget Grandad. "I'm off to find him and see if I can get back the page he tore out of *The Splotter's Guide To Cooking Up Trouble.*"

The Big Yin twins ran to the end of a short wooden pier and peered over the railings while Gadget Grandad waded into the water. He bobbed about like a yellow bath duck, clutching his brawsome bagpipes under one arm.

There was no sign of a boat to pull him along.

Just a great, grey triangle slicing through the icy waves!

The mighty grey fin dipped underwater until only the tip was showing, and whooshed towards Gadget Grandad as fast as you can read: *was he on today's menu?*

"Sh-sh-shark!" cried Isla, banging the railings to scare the fish away.

Mmmm. Fish.

"This is Walter," Gadget Grandad shouted to the twins on the shore. He grabbed the shark's fin tip and rose onto his long flippers. "Walter and I have been skiing together since we were nippers!"

"Is he still a nipper?" Ross spluttered.

"Sometimes. But Walter only gobbles other fish. He's *turbot-powered*!"

The mighty shark flicked its tail and pulled Gadget Grandad far out to sea, where he Walter-skied for the huge crowd of pensioners who had gathered on the beach with Isla and Ross. They waved the world's biggest banner that said:

WE LOVE GADGET GRANDAD!

Mavis Muckle and her elephant were in the crowd. "We're his biggest fins, I mean fans," chuckled Mavis. "We come here every Tuesday to watch the fin, I mean, fun."

Everyone OOOHED as Gadget Grandad Walter-skied on one leg and AAAHED when he Walter-skied upside-down on his head. He was getting further away.

"Looks like he's heading for that strange blue island," said Ross.

Mavis whipped a glass jam jar from her handbag and held it to her right eye.

"What can you see?" asked Isla.

"Jam," grumbled Mavis, scooping out a stubborn spoonful stuck in the jar. The glass bottom now magnified the view nicely. "That's nae island," she spluttered. "That's a blue whale as long as three buses – and the whale-weigh station says it's as heavy as three buses too!"

(The old lady was wise in the ways of whales and buses.)

What she didn't see was Fergus McFungus clinging to the back of the whale! I did, thanks to my *mega-super-well-OK-not-bad* cat vision.

The crowd left their banner and raced to the shoreline to get a better look. All eyes were on Gadget

Grandad, Walter and the whale, except two. Those two eyes belonged to a man who was fond of toadstools and trouble. And big abandoned banners left behind on beaches. (Which is not easy to say – or type.)

Big abandoned banners left behind on beaches.

Big abandoned banners left behind on beaches.

But wait...

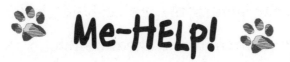 **Me-HELP!**

That man, Fergus McFungus, was steering the whale straight towards us!

11

All At Sea

The whale (and Fergus) ploughed towards the shore, with only Gadget Grandad and Walter in the way.

"We meet again!" cried Gadget Grandad. "Give me that secret secret recipe!"

"Never," growled Fergus, waving the page he had torn from the secret secret recipe book like a tiny white flag of surrender – but he wasn't surrendering, he was waving goodbye!

At that same moment, the blue whale was opening its mighty mouth. Its ginormous fishcakehole was about to swallow Gadget Grandad

– every bit, even his bald patch!

The twins couldn't look.

Nor could I, because I was getting out of Fergus's way. The whale had blasted him into the sky on a jet of water and he was heading straight for the beach.

SPLOSH!

I dived into the sea! (I was OK, I love the sea. It's full of fish. I just wish it was a bit drier.)

 Me-drip

Meanwhile Gadget Grandad was OK too. He'd wailed a warning on his bagpipes to scare the whale off. The whale wailed back and dived out of sight, creating a giant wave! As the water spalooshed over Gadget Grandad, he let go of Walter and bobbed back up on his bagpipes. He floated gently towards us and grinned. "Saved by the bagpipes!"

Me-phew

We dripped up the beach and were met by Mavis Muckle, who was jumping up and down on one wheelchair wheel because she was hopping mad and liked hopping.

"Someone's burgled our banner!" she said, wobbling furiously.

"It was Fergus McFungus," sighed Ross. "I saw him running off the beach with it."

"Why would he need a giant cloth?" asked Isla. "If only we knew which recipe he took from that book."

"He's cooking up something terrible, sure as bad eggs are bad eggs," said Gadget Grandad. "The big question is... what will he nab next?"

"Probably an elephant, like my Basil," Mavis piped up. "*Everyone* wants an elephant."

12

Wonderful Wednesday

The next morning, Isla put a drop of milk in my bowl for breakfast.

Just one teensy weensy drop.

"Sorry, Porridge," she sighed. "Gadget Grandad didn't know you were coming to stay."

One lick and the drop was gone. I grumbled under my breath and my hungry tum grumbled under my coat. Before we could moan any more, Gadget Grandad squeezed through the kitchen doorway, wearing five thick woolly jumpers, three hats and two pairs of gloves.

"Looks like snow is on the way," he said coolly. "Wrap up warm, you two."

The children stared up at the sunny blue sky, more puzzled than a million-piece jigsaw, but glad their wacky week was turning unexpectedly exciting.

A paragraph later, we all traipsed outside into the sunshine with our cosy coats on. My coat looked the best. Tartan is *always* in fashion, especially when I wear it.

"I received a distress signal from my old pal Archie," said Gadget Grandad. "And I think Fergus McFungus has got something to do with it." He led us to his garage and flung open the door.

"Welcome to my **N**o. **E**ffort. **S**uper. **S**aver. **I**n. **E**mergencies... mobile vehicle. Nessiemobile for short," the old man purred.

I purred too and hopped inside. The soft seats looked more comfortable than my cosy basket at home.

"This is megafabulificent!" said Ross, which was hard to say and even harder to spell.

"Why do you think Fergus McFungus is after Archie?" asked Isla as they sped away.

"Archie and I used to work undercover at a golf course. We were undercover because it rained a lot – and we were spies."

"*You* were a spy?" shouted Isla.

"A long time ago, aye. Archie and I bugged an underground bunker by the 18th green where **S.P.L.O.T.** agents liked to hide."

"What bugs did you use?" said Ross.

"Fleas mostly," said Gadget Grandad. "By the time

we finished bugging those **S.P.L.O.T.** agents, they were scratching like dugs!"

Me-arrgh

SCRATCH   **SCRATCH**   **SCRATCH**

Don't mention fleas!

Whenever anyone does, I start to scratch. (It's a cat thing.)

SCRATCH

We soon reached the edge of Tattiebogle Town and rumbled onwards through fields of amazing maize and corny corn, towards the shimmering waters of Loch Loch.

"Loch out for the look!" cried Ross, getting his murds wuddled.

But Gadget Grandad went straight for the water!

 Me-help!

I've already had enough WET on me for one book!
The Nessiemobile plunged into the murky wet
stuff and all was black – because I had my eyes
closed. Then we bobbed up like a cork. A pair of
lights on the long-necked scoop glowed like green
eyes and startled a group of tourists, who shrieked
and took blurry photos from the shore.

We wound down our windows to wave, and a
tasty salmon leapt right through mine and flopped
out the other window before I could catch it!

"Never mind, Porridge," said Isla. "Plenty more fish
in the sea – er, loch."

I'd rather the fish were in my tum.

13

Trouble Ahead!

The Nessiemobile sploshed through the shallows and trundled up the side of a pretty steep mountain, which was pretty and steep and a mountain.

As we climbed higher, a mischievous wind played with my fluffy fur, then got bored and played with Isla's fluffy hat instead. We passed a turning that said:

ARCHIE'S FARM

but we didn't stop.

"Archie took up farming when he retired, just like I took up gadgetry. He won't be at home just now though," said Gadget Grandad. "Every Wednesday he goes on a long mountain walk with his favourite coo, Morag."

Just then, a snowflake symbol flashed on the dashboard.

"A snowstorm is coming," muttered Gadget Grandad. "Hold on to your hats."

And your cats.

I peered out at a cloudless sky full of no clouds at all. Didn't look snowy to me.

"You're looking the wrong way, Porridge," said Isla.

"Aye, trouble ahead!" shouted Gadget Grandad.

I watched in mild horror (suitable for a family audience) as the amazing Nessiemobile rumbled into an icy blizzard. We frantically wound up our windows as a million billion trillion (and whatever the next big number is) snowflakes covered us in a thick white blanket.

"We need extra light," roared Gadget Grandad, jabbing a switch so his Nessiemobile glowed more brightly.

Two dazzling fog lamps revealed a ghostly white shape stumbling through the snow and whirling its arms so wildly I thought it would take off.

"It's abominable," squeaked Ross.

"It's Archie," said Gadget Grandad.

14

Snow Joking Around

"BRRRRRRRRRRRARGGGGH!"

Archie rumbled, shaking the snow off his bushy eyebrows and warming his hands by the Nessiemobile heaters. "Ye came just in time for me, but Morag – ma best coo – is missing!" He pinged a frozen tear from his eye. "And she's no' been milked! Poor Morag."

"We must find her," said Isla. "This snowstorm is getting worse."

"'Tis most unnatural for this time of year," said Archie.

"Aye, the last time there was a snowstorm in summer it was all the fault of Fergus McFungus," said

Gadget Grandad. "He built a snow machine to try and steal *The Splotter's Guide To Cooking Up Trouble*. It has to be him again."

"Maybe this snowstorm is to cover his tracks?" said Isla.

"Aye, 'tis certainly covering Morag's tracks," said Archie, with a shiver of regret.

The Nessiemobile rolled forward and its green lamps scanned the snow for clues. But they were no match for my *mega-super-well-OK-not-bad* cat's eyes: I honed in on half-hidden hoof prints ahead, which isn't easy to do or say. Try it.

Honed in on half-hidden hoof prints ahead.
Honed in on half-hidden hoof prints ahead.

So I just pointed them out with my tail.

"Nice one, Porridge," said Ross.

We were thundering down a steep slope, following the hoof prints, when I spotted a toadstool, teetering on the edge of a deep gully. We were heading straight towards it! Gadget Grandad braked and his Nessiemobile skidded to a stop.

Hmmm. Now we were teetering on the edge of a deep gully too.

"Nobody move except me," he warned, "I have an idea."

Gadget Grandad inflated his bagpipes with gulps of air. Soon the Nessiemobile was filled with the tartan bag – and I was squashed against the window like a furry fly.

He pointed its pipes out of the window and got us to hug the blown-up bag.

WHOOSH-WAIL-OOSH!

Three jets of air blasted us backwards, away from the gully. A musical moan lingered in the air.

 Me-phew!

"We must find Morag," said Archie.

Suddenly a mournful moo came out of the icy whiteness across the gully.

"We have!" whooped Gadget Grandad.

"That's ma girl!" Archie shouted, pointing to where they could just make out something stuck in a snowdrift on the other side of the steep drop. "Over there."

"I get your drift," said Gadget Grandad.

Poor Morag was **udderly** terrified and couldn't **moooove.**

"There's no bridge," said Ross. "How can we save her?"

"Nae worries," said Gadget Grandad. He jiggled a joystick and the Nessiemobile's long-armed scoop swung up into the swirling snowflakes.

Seven heartbeats went by before we saw it again, swinging back towards us, holding a snow-covered coo.

"Ye managed tae scoop Morag up as if she was dairy ice cream! Och aye the coo," said Archie, his heart leaping like a salmon on a pogo stick.

With Morag comfortably perched in the scooping arm at the front of the vehicle, Gadget Grandad threw the Nessiemobile into reverse and we slithered backwards, picking up speed.

We rumbled back down the rocky mountainside to the safety of Archie's milking shed.

Mmmm. Milk.

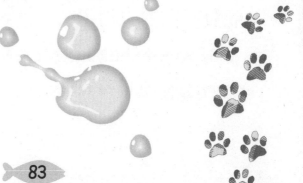

15

The Milk Goes Off

Now the danger was over, all Archie had to do was:

a) milk Morag, and

b) leave lots of milk in a bucket for any cat who might happen to be passing. Which today just so happened to be me.

Sadly, neither a) nor b) was possible.

"We found ma coo too late," he sighed. "I'm afraid Morag has already been milked by someone else. She's empty."

"So is your milk shed!" Gadget Grandad's voice echoed from a bare room.

"What?" Archie yelped in shock.

We all ran in and saw nothing but nothing!

"This morning ma warehoose was bursting with delicious farm produce!" moaned Archie. "All ma butter and eggs are gone!"

I yowled in thirst.

"Hold on a second," said Ross, kneeling down by a pointy toadstool lying on the floor, not daring to touch its pale blue skin. "What's this?"

"Step away. That is a poisonous BlatFlurble," warned Archie. "One touch and your fingers will turn orange and your hair go green with blue spots. It happened to me once and I was off-colour for a week."

"It means Fergus has been here," grumbled Gadget Grandad. "He's gone too far this time. First he stole a page from the recipe book, then a massive cloth banner, and now masses of Morag's milk, endless eggs and big boxes of butter."

"If only we knew what was on that torn-out page," said Isla.

"A recipe for disaster, I'm sure," said Archie.

"Udder mayhem," agreed Gadget Grandad. "My guess is Fergus still needs a shedload of other ingredients, and I know for a fact where he'll be tomorrow."

"Where?" said the twins.

"The Scottish Shed-Racing Championships," he declared. "Fergus McFungus and I have been battling for the title for years! He wouldn't miss it for the world, or for Scotland."

"We didn't know you raced sheds," said Ross.

"Only on Thursdays," said Gadget Grandad. "We cannot let Fergus be Champion. He will use the prize money to fund his evil plans!"

A silence fell over us, and I fell over it too.

"You look worried, Gadget Grandad," said Ross.

"Aye, I am," the old man replied wearily. "He's very good at being bad. His powerful shed is as big as a barn. In fact it *is* a barn, made of larch. He's my larch rival!"

They trudged back to the Nessiemobile in silence and shoes that squeaked a little (which was really annoying because it made me think there was a wee timorous mousie about).

Mmmm. Mouse.

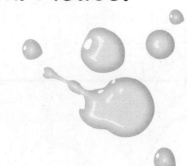

16

Thrilling Thursday

There was *still* no mouse or milk the next morning so Gadget Grandad popped round to see his neighbour in his pajamas. Innis Pajamas had a spare carton, which was lucky. Tasty too. Thanks Innis!

 **Me-yum!**

After an exhausting hundred laps of my milky bowl I was cat-tired and ready for a lie down.

BANG!

There was a terrifying noise. I shot in the air and landed in the sink, for the third time in this story.

"Poor Porridge," Isla giggled as she dried my dripping fur with a tea towel. "What was that, I wonder?"

BANG! BANG!

"It's coming from the shed at the bottom of the garden," said Ross.

We dashed off to investigate.

"Hello," said a faraway voice in faraway letters. Gadget Grandad slid from under the shed, wiping oil from his nose. "My shed won't start. If I don't fix it I can't stop Fergus McFungus from winning the Scottish Shed-Racing Championships!"

"Has it run out of petrol?" asked Ross.

"No. The Green Machine runs on water to protect the planet from pollution," explained Gadget Grandad.

I padded around the shed and spotted a deep puddle. I followed its wet trail to an empty barrel that was bolted on the back of the shed. A barrel with a big hole! I pointed out the problem with my tail.

"Clever Porridge," said Ross. "No wonder the shed won't start. It's sprung a leak!"

"Sprung a leek, more like," chuckled Gadget Grandad. "It's always popping out."

He plucked a soggy leek from the puddle and plugged the vegetable back in its hole. Then he refilled the barrel and they all hopped in. I'm hopeless at hopping so I catwalked in – showing off my terrific tartan coat to a jealous grey squirrel.

"This trusty rusty shovel is the brake," explained Gadget Grandad, "and this round dustbin lid is for steering round corners."

"What is this round biscuit tin for?" asked Isla.

"Fuelling *us* up, of course," said Gadget Grandad, taking out a chunk of shortbread. "Off we go!"

One minute and fifteen chunks later, we arrived at:

Flora's Garden Centre and Café
(and toilets but we don't mention them very much)

"Where's Fergus?" asked Isla.

"Right at the front," said Gadget Grandad.

"We need to track him closely today. He will definitely be up to *no good* (or *yes bad*, which is the same thing)."

We lined up behind nine rumbling sheds as Flora, who was 102 years old, swept the track with a broom and all the energy of a 101 year old.

"Fergus really wants to win," said Isla, peering over at his giant larch shed.

"I bet there is something else around here he wants too," said Ross.

And he was right. But I won't tell you just yet because that would ruin the story.

Suddenly the air was full of cheers and crumbs as Flora shook her gingham tablecloth and signaled the start of the race.

"Hold tight," shouted Gadget Grandad and we thundered away in a cloud of dust and dusty spiders.

17

Feeling Flat

What a great start. We rushed down the track and squeezed past three slower sheds. Then at Chicory Chicane we barrelled by two more competitors. It was all too easy.

"Five down, five to go," whooped Gadget Grandad.

He swung the Green Machine around a corner and clipped a bush (into the shape of me – braw!).

Ahead of us, a shed with pink-and-white *go-faster* stripes ahead of us screeched, struck a pothole and tipped on its side, scattering ~~cactuses~~ ~~cacti~~ ~~cactiuses~~, er, pointy plants in our path.

I screeched too and dived for the brake, shoving the shovel into the ground as we skidded towards the spiky plants. Sparks flew. Too late!

There was a pop and a hiss.

(And another hiss from me.)

We had a puncture. The Green Machine flubbered to a halt.

"We've three fat tyres and one flat one," sighed Isla.

"Aye, so we have tae lift the shed to change it," groaned Gadget Grandad. "But how?"

I figured it out because I'm clever. You're clever too. You must be, because you're reading this book.

Fergus was racing further away and we were in a hurry so I gave Gadget Grandad a wee clue. I jumped on his bagpipes, which wailed. (I wailed too and hid in a bush, trembling like a tartan leaf.) (I can be such a scaredy-cat sometimes.)

"Nice one, Porridge," said Gadget Grandad.

He slid his bagpipes under the shed and blew into them, deep and hard. They ballooned and the shed rose off the ground like a startled hippo. One sentence later, the flat tyre was fixed and we were back on track. A very bumpy track.

Gadget Grandad accelerated faster than I can typ...

"We're over halfway round," he said, "but here comes a tricky bamboo bend!"

I watched in astonishment as two bamboozled sheds lost control and clattered into a compost heap full of rotting vegetables. The air was filled with silence, then a-thousand-and-two rotten tomatoes

SPLAT.   SPLAT.   SPLATTED.

onto our rocking roof.

"This race is ace," whooped Isla.

"We're second!" cried Ross as we excitedly bucketed about like an excited bucket.

Och, what a race this was. The thundering tyres. The shouting fans. The cat falling off his seat onto a cactus.

 Me-OWCH!

That wasn't funny. I've got more prickles in my bahookie than a porcupine.

18

Thrilling Thursday Thunders On

I'm OK. I just need a wee tickle under the chin and a fishy biscuit or ten, or however many you have in your hand.

 **Me-yum!**

Back to the awesome action. Fergus McFungus stuck out a long smellyscope and swung it behind him. When he smelt how close we were, he frowned and yanked a yellow lever that opened a secret shed hatch.

Pots and pots of pots smashed on the track, blocking our way once again!

The spectators couldn't believe their eyes, so they watched a replay on a giant screen. Some even read about it in this book afterwards to make sure.

"That's cheating," said Herb McHerb sagely. "Fergus should have gone in for a pot stop if he wanted to lighten his load."

"He's breaking the rules," said Mavis Muckle, speaking sense.

And the pots, said Basil, speaking Elephant. (By the way, I understand Elephant fluently. I can speak six-hundred-and-forty-three languages including Mouse. Actually I squeak that.)

There was only one way to get past potty old Fergus. Gadget Grandad swung his steering lid and cried, "Let's cut him off at the parsley!"

The Green Machine took a shuddery short-cut through a shrubbery short-cut and hurtled across a herb garden. Herbs flew everywhere, except Herb McHerb who always took the bus. We whizzed past Rosemary and Basil and Clive who were picking rosemary and basil and some chives (which was close enough).

By the middle of this sentence we were back on track. There was nothing between us and Fergus in front. But then, a giant jet engine rose from his shed roof. Fergus hit a button marked FIRE and flames flew out the back of the engine.

FLAMBOOOOSSHHHH!

Now we were well and truly cooked! I felt the hairs on my head curling as Fergus McFungus's shed shot away like a red rocket over some green rocket, which is a tasty salad. You should try it.

Somewhere in the distance, Flora was *very* slowly pegging a wet tablecloth on the finish line. She didn't see Fergus McFungus approaching at a zillion scowls an hour...

"My larch rival has nearly won," said Gadget Grandad with a heavy heart, in heavy gardening boots. His shed was heavy too, and that was the problem. We needed to go faster!

Luckily, the old man had something up his sleeve.

A hairy wrist. And on the end of that hairy wrist was a handy fist that thumped on a button marked:

A mighty explosion of mega-hot mustard power erupted from our shed and we thundered towards Flora so fast she dropped her pegs in amazement and a puddle.

Now the two old school rivals were level pegging, racing their sheds side by side.

"You're super-doomed," snarled Fergus. With one twist of his joystick he slammed us sideways.

"Super-*zoomed* more like," roared Gadget Grandad. The herbo-boosted shed roared too. So did the excited crowd.

I somersaulted
onto Gadget Grandad's
baldy head and clung
on like a bad wig.

Whoooooosshhhh!

That was the sound of the Green Machine as it
flew over the finish line in first place!

"We did it!" cried the twins.

"Very jammy," I heard Fergus shouting as he swerved around Flora into a stack of very jammy scones.

And that was that –

19

Scone Or Gone?

(Fergus's crash spattered jam and scones everywhere, so I apologise if a few pages stick together when you're reading this.)

"Fergus McFungus sure came to a sticky end," said Isla, licking some jam off her nose.

"I'm not so sure," said Gadget Grandad, spying a trail of smashed scones that led all the way to the next paragraph.

I didn't need my *mega-super-well-OK-not-bad* cat vision to spot what fiendish trickery Fergus McFungus had been up to. His sticky fingerprints were all over Flora's now-bare café. He must have tossed sacks and sacks of sacks into his big shed and vanished in a cloud of flour and mixed fruit.

"Och, all my sultanas and raisins and flour and soda have gone!" Flora spluttered, nibbling on her last scone. She spluttered again because it was a wee bit dry.

Me-yuck!

Gadget Grandad paced up and down the empty room, deep in thought and jam. "Tomorrow we must stop Fergus once and for all! I fear he now has all the ingredients to bake something so earth-shatteringly awful that it will destroy **THE WORLD AND VOLCANOES AND FISHY BISCUITS.**"

And elephants. Never forget elephants because they never forget you.

He bundled us into the Green Machine and drove home in time for supper. There's always time for supper in my book. (And this *is* my book, I'm only lending it to you. Check at the front if you don't believe me.)

Plus, I needed more fishy biscuits. After all, I'd only eaten that handful you snuck me ages and pages ago.

Sleepy now, I lay on the windowsill, bathed in blue moonlight and saw a shooting star in the sky. Oddly, it shot up, not down, and blazed a fiery trail across the sky.

I yawned.

Friday beckoned.

Fergus McFungus was about to stir up Trouble with a capital T. He was going to need a very big bowl!

20

Far-out Friday

Early Friday morning, the twins heard a loud squeaking on the landing and sprang out of bed to investigate. I did too.

"Sounds like a giant mouse," said Isla.

Mmmm. Mouse.

Ross crept onto the landing with a rolled-up comic in his hand.

"Are you going to teach it to read?" giggled Isla.

"Very funny," he said, swishing the comic under the bookcase. "Nothing down there."

"It might be in the loft," said Isla, pointing to a trapdoor in the ceiling.

As they looked up, it slowly and squeakily began lowering like a ramp on an alien spaceship. Ross stumbled back in surprise, landing on the landing.

"I've been expecting you," boomed a mysterious figure in a shiny silver spacesuit. He slid up his gold face visor to reveal a one-eyed alien called Frank.

Just kidding.

"It's only me," said Gadget Grandad, who wasn't a one-eyed alien called Frank after all. We clambered into the loft, and I curled up on a comfy sofa made from the back seat of an old car.

Around us, funky bulbs swirled and chunky dials whirled, and in the middle of all this computerised chaos Gadget Grandad flitted about like a moth at a twinkling funfair.

"Nearly ready," he said, bending a coat hanger to make an aerial for his spacesuit.

"Where did you get your intergalactic gear?" asked Isla.

"I made it," Gadget Grandad called back, "but first I sent a smaller suit into space. It worked perfectly with its wee jam-jar helmet."

He held up the silver test suit. It was no bigger than me and it looked warm and cosy, so I climbed in.

"That suit suits you, Porridge," chuckled Ross.

Gadget Grandad beckoned us into a huddle. "Let me explain why we are in the loft. Last night I couldnae sleep so I tried to play a lullaby on my bagpipes but they were blocked. I blew harder and guess what shot out?"

"What?" chimed the twins.

"*The Splotter's Guide To Cooking Up Trouble!*"

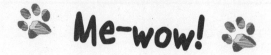

"It must have been sucked up with the spies!" gasped Ross.

Gadget Grandad opened the battered book. "The bad news is: Fergus tore out page 99, the deadliest page in the book. The good news is: we still have the contents page at the front, so we can work out what his plans might be."

He ran a finger down the contents list.

"A clootie dumpling!" giggled the twins. "What's so deadly about that? Dad makes them all the time."

"Not as big as this one," warned Gadget Grandad. "Think of all the ingredients Fergus has filched. No wonder he stole that giant banner when I was Walter-skiing – he had to have a clootie rag big enough to cook it in. His clootie dumpling will be huge – too huge to hide here on Earth! Last night I saw something launch into the sky. It looks like we don't have much time."

Och, I saw it too!

Isla had a question. "What is Fergus McFungus up to?"

"The Moon, by now." Gadget Grandad chuckled at his own joke. "Our mission today is to race into space and save the world and volcanoes and fishy biscuits and elephants."

"We don't have a rocket," said Ross.

"We don't need one." Gadget Grandad patted a white cube with small silver panels. "We have this."

Isla carefully examined the object. She concluded it was a solar-powered bread maker.

"Aye, but it disnae just make bread any more," said Gadget Grandad.

"What else does it do?" Isla asked, curious as a cat.

(So was I, because I'm a cat.)

"Lift-off!" chuckled Gadget Grandad. "When its yeasty bubbles pop they will shoot this loft into space! And you'll be the first twins in orbit together! Och, I've already put in my super-strong yeast mixture, so there isn't a moment to lose. Buckle up, kids! It's going to be a bumpy ride!"

"Do we need spacesuits like you and Porridge?" asked Ross.

"No, no, you'll be fine as you are in the airtight loft."

Grandad jabbed a button to retract the ramp and shut the steel door to make everything airtight. In seconds, the bread maker began counting down in seconds.

10. 9. 8.

The whole loft jugglebuggled...

7. 6. 5. 4.

flizzerlubbled...

3. 2. 1.

and
blasted

OFF!

Mavis Muckle was walking Basil
by the house when she heard a
tremendous

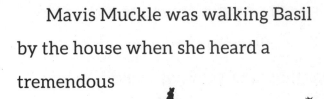

whoosh!

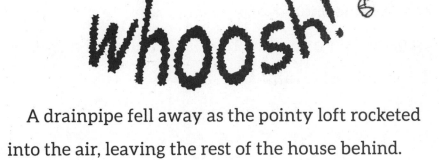

A drainpipe fell away as the pointy loft rocketed

into the air, leaving the rest of the house behind.

Bursting with excitement, she watched the yeast bubbles burst with excitement.

Soon all she could see of the roof was a wee dot just like this one.

"Och, there goes the roof," she muttered to Basil. "I hope it disnae rain."

21

Far Far Out Friday

What a glorious glibblefribbling ride it was into space, full of crazy loops and words and finally, at the end of this long sentence, there was a mighty

DING!

Then all was quiet and the air was full of silence and freshly baked bread.

"Och, we made it," said Gadget Grandad. "The launch is the hard part. Floating safely in space is a weight off my mind."

"And the rest of you," giggled Ross.

"I can fly like an eagle," whooped Isla, flapping up to the ceiling then down to the carpet.

"The eagle has landed," chuckled Gadget Grandad.

"Right, we're looking for Fergus. He'll be somewhere big enough to mix a giant mixture."

He somersaulted onto the sofa and pulled a periscope down from the ceiling. It was made from a long plastic pipe and lots of old pairs of glasses. The far end keeked out of the chimney like a shy Santa and swiveled as Gadget Grandad glanced about.

"Let's take a look at the Man In The Moon. His left eye is an old crater," he said, fiddling a dial to get the image less blurry. "My guess is Fergus will use the crater as a mixing bowl and cover it with the giant clootie banner he stole while I was Walter-skiing. Then he will bake everything rock hard in the rays of the sun."

When the crater came into focus, Gadget Grandad bounced off the sofa in shock and tartan slippers.

"What's wrong?" asked Isla.

"The crater is empty! Fergus must have already taken his clootie dumpling off the Moon to cool down in space!" He rushed to the window. "Behold! A super-sized suet pudding set to collide with Planet Earth!"

The twins gawped like goldfish as soon as they saw it.

Mmmm. Goldfish.

"It's amazing," said Ross.

"It's moving," said Isla.

"It's a meteor," warned Gadget Grandad, "full of peril and sultanas! In two minutes it will shoot past us and plummet to Earth."

"If only we could hit it out of the way," said Isla.

"I'd need a bigger comic," sighed Ross, swishing his so hard he burst a milk carton and a delicious white weightless blob bobbled out.

I spun my tail like a propeller and floated towards the milky treat.

Mmmm. Milk.

 ## Me-slurp

Unable to stop moving, I bounced against Gadget Grandad's brawsome bagpipes and rebounded out of control. Isla dived to her left and caught me like a furry football.

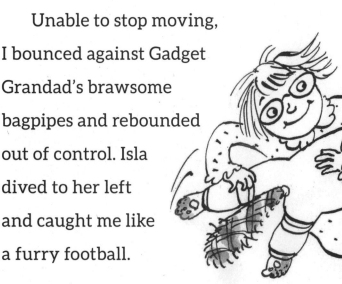

"That catapulted cat has given me an idea," cried Gadget Grandad, flipping down his gold visor and slipping on two seaside flippers. "With a bit of luck – and a lot of bounce – my bagpipes can boing the clootie dumpling away from Earth! You're a genius, Porridge!"

Aye, I am!

22

Dumpling Danger

Gadget Grandad connected the bread maker to his bagpipes with a stretchy vacuum-cleaner hose. He filled the machine with yeast and carried everything to the ramp.

"You cannae breathe in space, so while I'm out here in my space suit you've got to keep the loft airtight." Grandad's voice crackled through a tinny helmet speaker cannily made from a tin can. "Lock the door after me."

The twins shut the steel door to the airlock and lowered the ramp, then Gadget Grandad

somersaulted into space. We rushed to the window to see him float by and turn the machine up to full.

A stream of yeasty bubbles bobbled through the long hose into the bagpipes, which gobbled them greedily and doubled in size.

Then doubled once more.

Then again and again.

Soon Gadget Grandad was a wee silver speck beside a huge tartan blob. Still it grew.

Suddenly I saw a chilling sight – so chilling it cooled my blood and a nearby flask of tea. The deadly clootie dumpling was close now. It was as big as the biggest thing you can imagine, and it was picking up speed (because of gravy or gravity or something). A ragged clootie rag streamed behind it.

The stupendous suet comet streaked past the window and missed us by a whisker.

🐾 Me-phew 🐾

But the danger wasn't over! All at once the loft shuddered and started to move. It was being dragged through the inky darkness by the comet!

"That pesky clootie rag has snagged on the chimney!" warned Gadget Grandad through his visor radio. "It must be cut free!"

"It's dragging us like a fish on a line!" yelled Ross.

Mmmm. Fish.

"Someone has to go outside," said Isla. "Gadget Grandad's already reached the clootie dumpling."

I was already wearing a wee space suit and jam jar helmet. So it had to be me! It was time to save the day – and the world!

I needed a way to cut up the clootie and spotted the answer in a box of junk. Groovy Gran's old false teeth!

I picked them up and bounced into the airlock.

"Good luck, Porridge!" said Ross, closing the door behind me.

I didn't hear him as I had jam in my ears. The ramp quickly lowered and I saw the Earth spinning before me like a muddy blue ball.

 **Me-wow!**

I climbed up the steep roof like a mountaineer climbing Everest (which was now just a pimple on the Earth's bahookie).

At the top of the roof, I spotted the problem. One end of the Clootie rag was wrapped around the chimney, too tight to unwind. I clacked the false teeth like a castanet and swiftly chopped the cloth in two.

Me-phew!

The loft spun away, free at last.

"Well done, that cat," crackled Gadget Grandad. "Time for my bagpipes to BOING that dumpling away from Earth."

He detached the hose...

BLUBBLEOOOSSSHHHH!

...and the **BRAWSOME BAGPIPES** jetted towards the **DASTARDLY DUMPLING**. I've just invented those nicknames, cool eh?

I clung to the chimney and crossed my tail for good luck.

3...

2...

1...

The **BRAWSOME BAGPIPES** struck the **DASTARDLY DUMPLING**! For one brief moment they both embraced like giant sumo wrestlers. Then the **BRAWSOME BAGPIPES**

boinged

the **DASTARDLY DUMPLING** back the way it had come.

Off it zoomed – straight back to the Moon – into the crater – and onto a larch shed. And that was the moment Fergus McFungus got his just desserts.

Och, and a very sore head!

23

Just In Time!

"Porridge!" yelled Isla. "You've got to get back on board quickly."

"You too, Gadget Grandad," roared Ross.

While I pulled myself towards the airlock ramp, the old man waited anxiously for the loft to spin near him. As quick as he could, in slow-motion, he inched up the ramp and dawdled to safety. It started to close automatically behind him.

"Where's Porridge?" said Ross.

Here, I hissed, floating through the closing gap.

Two gloved hands pulled me inside —

CLANG!

Just in time! Gadget Grandad cuddled me like a much-loved tartan teddy bear.

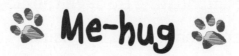 Me-hug

The twins hurriedly let us in.

"You saved the day," they whooped.

"Porridge," said Gadget Grandad, "is the bravest tartan cat I've ever seen."

Aye, that's because I'm the only one.

"Do you think anyone on Earth noticed the deadly dumpling danger?" asked Isla.

"Doesn't look like it" muttered Ross, peering down at the wee round ball. "It's just an ordinary Friday for them."

"And for me," chuckled Gadget Grandad.

"We've foiled Fergus for now."

"Will he be back?" asked Ross.

The old man shrugged, "Who knows?"

Well *I* do actually, and I'm not going to tell Gadget Grandad, or the twins – or you – that fiendish Fergus will probably maybe definitely turn up again. It's my wee secret.

Er, did I just tell you?

 ## Me-oops

OK – don't tell anyone else. Not even your brother or sister or your imaginary friend or a dug. NEVER tell a dug any secrets because it will bark them to every other dug in town at twilight, every night, forever!

Maybe longer.

24

The Last Chapter

After breakfast the next day, the twins picked up their rucksacks to go home and we joined Gadget Grandad by the front gate. He was perched on a homemade trandem bicycle, which boasted three wheels and three saddles.

"Look, three sets of pedals," said Ross.

"Enough for those of us with two legs," said Gadget Grandad. "Porridge can sit in the front basket."

I leapt in – no pedalling for me. The wobbly contraption was soon whizzing through the streets, picking up speed and funny looks. Gadget Grandad

fell off outside the opticians, but that was ok because
he needed new glasses anyway.

"I'm a bit rusty," he explained.

"So is this bike," said Isla.

We rattled home as fast as their legs could carry me.

Mum opened the door because we don't have a cat
flap or a twins flap.

"Did you have a nice time?" she asked in that
Did-you-have-a-nice-time? mum-voice that mums do.

"It was brilliant!" said Ross.

"The best week ever!" added Isla.

Mum was so surprised her mouth fell open and
she swallowed a wee midgie.

Gadget Grandad tickled my ears. "Now you know

why I don't do anything on Sundays," he said to the twins. "I need a wee rest after an adventurous week."

"We'd really very much definitely love to come round more often," said Isla.

Ross nodded urgently in agreement.

A magical smile crinkled Gadget Grandad's face. "Maybe Gran can take you out with her next time? Her awesome adventures really rock!"

Ross hopped like excited popcorn. "What does she do?"

"Last week she popped out to get ice for her lemonade."

"Where?" asked Isla.

"The North Pole!"

Isla gasped. "That's incredibly cool!"

"Exactly," chuckled Gadget Grandad.

This news was just what the children wanted to hear. Things would never be boring again, apart from electric drills and woodworm.

When he was halfway down the road, Gadget Grandad was still waving and saying, "See you soon!"

Slowly he cycled out of sight – and this story. But it was nearly the end anyway so that's OK.

There was just enough space at the end of the chapter for Ross and Isla to find me a fishy biscuit treat.

 Me-yum-yum-yum-yum!

I love fishy biscuits.

CAT

Be your own tripewriter
and unjumble these words:

1. DIGRO~~P~~R~~E~~
   P _ _ _ _ _ _ E

2. G~~S~~~~Y~~AI~~O~~PE
   B _ _ P _ _ _ S

3. ~~T~~E~~O~~GDA
   G _ _ _ _ _ T

4. HL~~T~~~~Z~~NE~~P~~A
   E _ _ _ P _ _ _ _ T

5. AN~~O~~~~J~~~~Y~~OCL
   V _ _ _ _ _ _ O

And here are some of my favourite jokes...

What do cats read in the morning?

A *mew*spaper!

What shoes do spies wear on their feet?

Sneakers!

Why can't big cats take a test?

Too many cheetahs!

Why are elephants so wrinkled?

Have you ever tried to iron one?

Read on for a sneaky peek
at my next topsy-turvy,
tartan-tastic, purrfectly crazy
adventure

Porridge the Tartan Cat
and the Bash-Crash-Ding

One morning, Ross heard a terrifying growl outside the back door.

GRRRRR!

"What was that?" he cried, hiding under the kitchen table.

"That was Porridge growling like a wee dug," giggled Isla.

It wasn't all of me, just my grumpy belly roaring, *FEED ME NOW!* I was outside and my food was inside, so I dashed hungrily towards the cat flap —

THWUMP!

Then I remembered there wasn't one.

🐾 Me-owch! 🐾

Ross opened the door and peeled me off it with his fingers and a sigh (but mostly with his fingers). He took me inside and soon I was doing my morning exercises – one hundred laps of a milky cat bowl.

🐾 Me-licious! 🐾

The twins were on the lookout for Gran. She was coming to stay with us because Mum and Dad were going on holiday.

"I can't see her anywhere," said Isla, at the window.

Gadget Grandad would have come too, but this morning he had to go on a secret mission. So secret that I'm not allowed to tell you about it, even in tiny letters.

"Gran always arrives with the same old trolley, wearing the same old clothes," said Ross.

"Gran does *everything* the same old way," groaned his sister. "She's stuck in a groove. She's stuck in a groove. She's..."

"Groovy Gran," giggled Ross.

At the end of their street and this sentence, Groovy Gran appeared, tugging her stubborn trolley. "It's stuck in a groove!"

The twins ran to help. (I would have lent a hand too, but as I don't have any I leant on the gatepost instead and watched.)

They yanked the trolley free, then Groovy Gran gave the twins a bony hug.

As they arrived at the front gate, Groovy Gran's bright eyes swept over my stripes like a barcode scanner. She bent down to give me a cuddle too, her joints cracking like fireworks.

Me-help!

Luckily for me, the front door opened and Mum and Dad came out, each carrying a big suitcase.

"See you next week," they cried, stuffing the suitcases into the car boot. "Have fun with Gran!"

They jumped in and set off, waving out of the windows.

Groovy Gran dragged her trolley to the front door, desperate for a cup of tea. "Kids, I'm making you something delicious later."

Ross and Isla looked at each other nervously.

"But... er..." said Isla.

"Aye, plenty of *butter* in your tattie scones."

The twins shuddered. Groovy Gran made tattie scones *every time* she came round. EVERY TIME!

"I need one extra thing," added Groovy Gran. "What's the word now...? You put it on porridge..."

"A collar?" joked Ross, looking at me.

Nope! I knew the answer, because I'm officially the cleverest cat in this story. See?

PORRIDGE IS OFFICIALLY
THE CLEVEREST CAT
IN THE WHOLE OF THIS STORY

– signed _____
Porridge the Tartan Cat

OK, I'm the only cat in this story... but I'm still
clever. The answer was: salt. To show the others,
I grabbed a shaker with my tartan tail and...

Groovy Gran vanished in a cloud of black pepper.

🐾 Me-oops 🐾

She sneezed —

BLA-CHOOOOW!!

And her false teeth shot out!

"Where are ma wallies?" she spluttered. (Groovy Gran calls false teeth 'wallies'.)

I couldn't see them, but...

...I could feel them biting ma bahookie!

How many tattie scones will
Isla and Ross have to eat?

Will Groovy Gran play with
her rock band again?

And what's the Dug o Doom
got to do with anything?

Find out in...

Porridge the
Tartan Cat
and the Bash-Crash-Ding